The Flame of Peace

**A TALE
OF THE AZTECS**

W9-BXY-547

jaguar

feathered serpent

blanket

eagle

stars

coyote

fruit and sweet potatoes

basket of cocoa seeds

pots of indigo dye

quetzal bird

fox

quetzal-feather headdress

rain frogs

flowers

deer

speech or song scrolls

net for fishing

roses

reed boat

rattlesnake

bee

chicken

potted cedar trees

sun

merchants

city wall

singers

dancers

parrot

scorpion

altar

turtle

centipede

rabbit

cactus

incense bag

turkey

torch

wasp

priestess

priest

copal,
used for offerings

corn cakes

obsidian-tipped spear

bowl of maize
soup

shield

sandal

eagle warrior

jaguar warrior

pipe

necklace

warrior's
nose plug

earplug

olin,
sign for earthquake

conch shell
for sounding the alarm

battle emblem

The Flame of Peace

A TALE OF THE AZTECS

DEBORAH NOURSE LATTIMORE

HarperTrophy
A Division of HarperCollins Publishers

The Flame of Peace
Copyright © 1987 by Deborah Nourse Lattimore
Printed in Mexico. All rights reserved.

Library of Congress Cataloging-in-Publication Data
Lattimore, Deborah Nourse.
The flame of peace.

Summary: To prevent the outbreak of war, a young
Aztec boy must outwit nine evil lords of the night
to obtain the flame of peace from Lord Morning Star.
   1. Aztecs—Juvenile fiction.   [1. Aztecs—Fiction.
2. Indians of Mexico—Fiction]   I. Title.
PZ7.L36998Fl 1987   [Fic]   86-26934
ISBN 0-06-023708-2
ISBN 0-06-023709-0 (lib. bdg.)
ISBN 0-06-443272-6 (pbk.)

For Steve
and Nicholas, Isabel, and Judith

Thanks to Linda Zuckerman, Sue Alexander, Katherine King,
and Edward Mitchell for help and encouragement.

Once a great, long time ago, the capital of the Valley of Mexico had another name. It was called Tenochtitlán, Land of the Aztecs. Bustling marketplaces brimmed with people. Merchants traded in the sunny plazas. In gleaming temples priests made offerings. And even though we do not know as much as we would like about the Aztecs, we do know about their art, their gods, their wars, and their hopes for peace.

There was once a boy called Two Flint, who fished in the sparkling lake outside the city walls. Two Flint knew of no better place on earth.

One day, Two Flint saw battle flags fluttering on the towers. Warriors stood along the walls. Emperor Itzcoatl himself appeared before the temple, draped in his imperial robes.

"Tezozomoc and his army are in the hills," the Emperor said. "He plans to capture our city. We must prepare ourselves. We will send ambassadors with gifts. Then we will see what kind of enemies these men are."

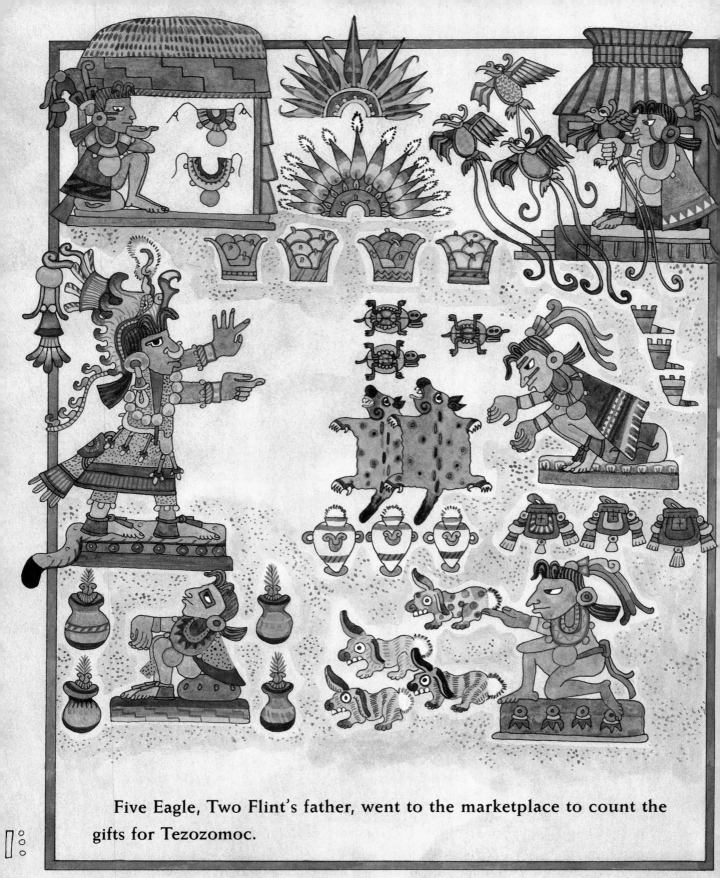

Five Eagle, Two Flint's father, went to the marketplace to count the gifts for Tezozomoc.

"Why do we send gifts to our enemies?" asked Two Flint.

"For the Twenty Days of Talking," answered Five Eagle. "We will show Tezozomoc how great we are by sending him our best things."

"Will there be peace after the Twenty Days?" asked Two Flint.

"Maybe peace. Maybe war," his father said. "Who knows? We have been enemies for many years."

The next morning Five Eagle stood in front of the temple with the other ambassadors. Priestesses danced before the stairs as smoke curled up from incense burners. Conch shells sounded from tower to tower. The Emperor raised his arms. The ambassadors saluted him.

"One day you may have to search for peace, Two Flint," said his father. "Be brave when that day comes!" Then he marched from the city.

For twenty days and twenty nights, Two Flint climbed the towers and squinted at the road leading to the hills. At last, ragged and limping figures appeared, but the father of Two Flint was not among them. Tezozomoc's warriors had taken his life.

"Let us prepare for war," said the Emperor. "Tezozomoc has broken the Twenty Days of Talking." He spilled copal juice down his face and right arm. "Tomorrow we face our enemy!"

Later, at home, Two Flint and his mother, One Flower, talked sadly.

"Did we always fight the people from the shores of Lake Texcoco?" Two Flint asked.

"Oh, no," she said. "Once the sacred light of the Morning Star burned in our temples and we were all brothers. But now the fire is dying. With no New Fire from Lord Morning Star, there can be no peace, only war."

"Where is Lord Morning Star?" asked Two Flint.

"There is a long road beyond the great city walls ruled by nine evil demons of darkness. At the end of the road is the Hill of the Star. That is where they say Lord Morning Star can be found. But all who have ever searched for him were soon lost." His mother shook her head.

The night, like a burning obsidian bowl, glowed with the flickering torches of foot runners as the city prepared for war. Temple altars blazed with fiery offerings of incense. Conch shells and bone whistles sang from the towers. At the House of Singing, warriors drank their favorite maize porridge, perhaps for the last time. Some sang while others danced a dance of war.

"If the New Fire burned in the great temple," Two Flint thought, "we would have peace. Tomorrow I will find Lord Morning Star and tell him we need his light!"

Two Flint's mind was made up. As he slept, he dreamed that the summer skies whirled their clouds around the moon. Lord Morning Star burst through the circle of moonlight. He spoke to Two Flint.

"Fight the nine evil ones, Two Flint," Lord Morning Star said. "But use your wits, not your sword! I wait for you! Come! Come!"

The next morning, the mighty Aztec army, weapons shining in the dazzling sunlight, marched away on the road to the hills. On the long mountain road, a single Aztec boy set off for the Hill of the Star.

"Two Flint!" called One Flower. "Why are you leaving?"

"My father told me to be brave and to search for peace," he answered.

"Then," One Flower said, "you must go."

The pale maize sun of dawn was hot amber when Two Flint came to
the crossroads, where the first evil demon awaited him.

"Go back!" growled a voice. "I am Crossroads, and no one passes me!"

"Mighty Lord Crossroads," said Two Flint, "I seek one greater than you!" Two Flint crossed his arms over his chest and stood tall.

"Greater than I?" said Crossroads. "I, who can change the path of River?" His arms whipped up and down, faster and faster until the banks of River shook.

"Lord River! Greater than Lord Crossroads!" called Two Flint, running to the riverbank. "Wash away all but the true road!"

"I am greater than Crossroads," gurgled Lord River. He dove deep into the riverbed and filled his mouth with water. Suddenly a giant waterspout swept away Lord Crossroads.

Two Flint jumped past River, but water was filling the road.

"Great Lord Wind!" called Two Flint, his heart beating wildly.
"Mightier than Lord River! Blow Lord River back!"

"Wind always blows stronger than River's current!" a howling, airy voice whistled. Over Two Flint's head a gust of wind blew, in torrents, in streams, in mighty bursts, pushing River back into his bed.

Two Flint climbed the steep riverbank, but Lord Wind blew him down.

"You fooled Crossroads and River," howled Lord Wind, "but you can't fool me!"

"Perhaps I am not powerful enough to fool you, mighty Wind," called Two Flint, "but look! Lord Storm has passed by you!" And he pointed ahead on the road to huge, gloomy, black clouds.

Lord Wind turned dark blue as he puffed up his cheeks and blew a giant gale. But Storm's frogs opened their mouths. Hail and rain flew like arrows across the sky, and the frogs swallowed Lord Wind.

Two Flint's legs shook and wobbled as he scrambled up the road. Lord
Storm passed behind. The ground ahead crumbled and cracked.
"Go back! No one passes Earthquake!" rumbled a voice below.
Two Flint grabbed the trunk of an old, gnarly tree.

"If you are so powerful, why is Lord Volcano taller than you?" Two Flint yelled.

The voice grumbled. Two Flint pressed himself tightly against the tree. Lord Earthquake roared and shook. The ground rippled through the tree's roots and split the bark.

"Lord Volcano!" Two Flint shouted. "Let Lord Earthquake shake the ground to pieces! You can put them back together!"

Smoke and ash filled the air. Lord Volcano poured out his fire and the rocks melted together.

"You passed ahead of Storm and you escaped Earthquake," bellowed Lord Volcano, "but you can't fool me!" Down poured his rocky fire.

Two Flint climbed from the tree to a cave high on a cliff. He held his breath as fiery rocks tumbled everywhere. When Lord Volcano stopped, the entrance was blocked. Two Flint was trapped.

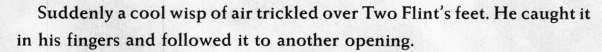

Suddenly a cool wisp of air trickled over Two Flint's feet. He caught it in his fingers and followed it to another opening.

"Go no farther!" thundered a voice outside. "I am Lord Smoking Mirror, the great trickster, and no one passes me without first holding my cloak!" A shadow larger than the sky darkened the road.

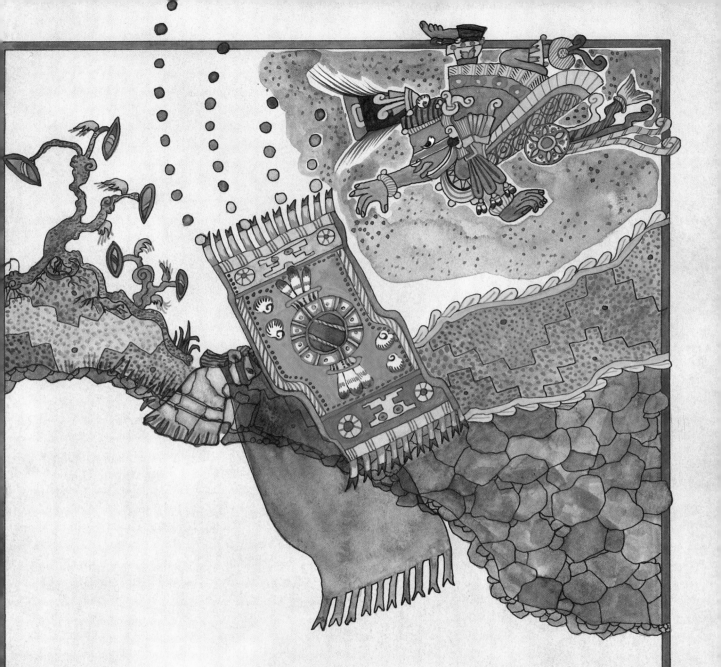

Two Flint knew that of all Lord Smoking Mirror's tricks, his cloak of forgetfulness was the most powerful. Quickly, Two Flint gathered together a pile of rocks and made a statue of himself. He pushed it out the opening. Down swooped the demon and dropped his cloak over the statue and flew away. Two Flint had tricked him.

His heart pounding hard and loud, Two Flint ran up the road until he came to a thick mist filled with the sounds of gnashing teeth and clattering bones. Out sprang the Lord and Lady of Death.

"Approach, Spirit! Now you belong to us!" they hissed, shaking their bones.

"Step back!" shouted Two Flint. "I am still alive! I fooled seven lords. You have power over the dead. But you have no power over me!" Faster than the jaguar, he shot up a steep hill and bolted through the clouds.

Spicy incense and flowers perfumed the air. Billowy clouds sparkled brighter than all the Emperor's jewels. Two Flint was on the top of the Hill of the Star.

"You have struggled long and hard, Two Flint," said a deep, calm voice. High over the mist appeared Lord Morning Star, bathed in silvery rays of moonlight. Glistening gold flames encircled him.

"In your search for peace, fighting with only your wits, you have found me. You are the new One of Peace, Prince Two Flint. Take the New Fire!" A brilliant flame on a feathery torch tumbled down to Two Flint.

Two Flint found himself running on the road toward Tenochtitlán, the
New Fire glimmering in his hands. Behind him Lord Morning Star shone,
spreading rays of red and gold across the sky.

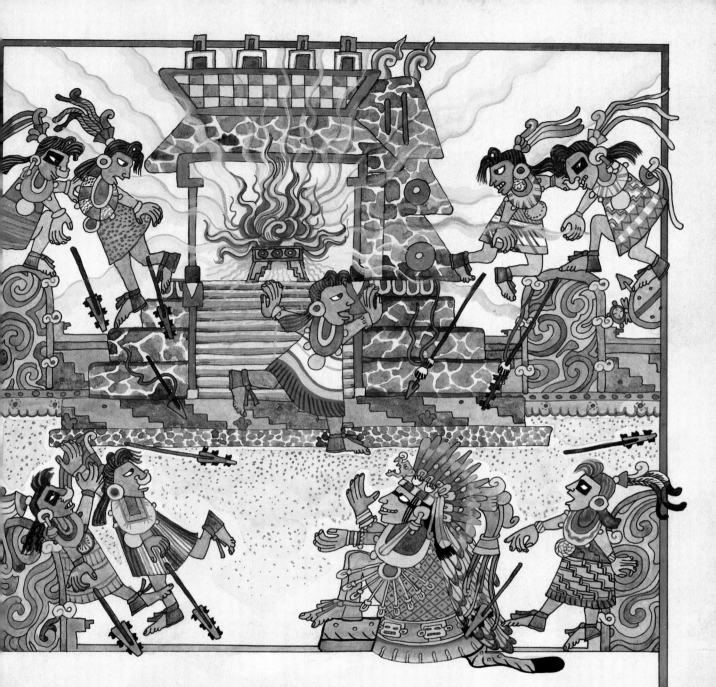

All along the walls, warriors who had fought their way into the city threw down their weapons and greeted Two Flint. Emperor Itzcoatl himself welcomed Two Flint as he climbed the stairs of the great temple and placed the New Fire on the altar.

"Let all fighting end!" Two Flint announced. "From this day on, let our city be a brother to all cities!"

That evening the people sang and danced. Itzcoatl's warriors and Tezozomoc's warriors broke their spears and embraced as friends.

Deep inside the temple, the glow of a single fire burned bright and true.

We know that the Aztecs feared nine evil lords of darkness and believed in a god of peace. Could a boy have outwitted those evil lords and struck a New Fire of peace from the Morning Star? All we know is that during the time of Itzcoatl, a great Alliance of Cities marked the beginning of many peaceful decades.

parrot

scorpion

altar

turtle

centipede

rabbit

cactus

incense bag

turkey

torch

wasp

priestess

priest

copal, used for offerings

corn cakes

obsidian-tipped spear

bowl of maize soup

shield

sandal

pipe

eagle warrior

jaguar warrior

necklace

warrior's nose plug

earplug

olin, sign for earthquake

conch shell for sounding the alarm

battle emblem